A Bad T

Elizabeth and Jessica tiptoed into the *Animal Hour* studio and hurried up to the seats where they had watched the show.

Just then, Dr. Snapturtle walked onto the stage. His dog, Duke, was trotting behind him, wagging his tail. Duke saw the piece of fish that had spilled from the bucket and picked it up in his mouth.

Dr. Snapturtle turned around and saw what Duke was doing. "Put that down!" he yelled.

Elizabeth froze. There was no reason for Dr. Snapturtle to scold Duke so strongly.

"That was mean," she finally blurted out.

Dr. Snapturtle glanced up and noticed the twins for the first time.

Then Jessica and Elizabeth dashed out of the studio.

Bantam Skylark Books in the
SWEET VALLEY KIDS series

SWEET VALLEY KIDS

ELIZABETH MEETS HER HERO

Written by
Molly Mia Stewart

Created by
FRANCINE PASCAL

Illustrated by
Ying-Hwa Hu

A BANTAM SKYLARK BOOK®
NEW YORK · TORONTO · LONDON · SYDNEY · AUCKLAND

RL 2, 005–008

ELIZABETH MEETS HER HERO
A Bantam Skylark Book / April 1992

*Sweet Valley High® and Sweet Valley Kids are
trademarks of Francine Pascal*

Conceived by Francine Pascal

*Produced by Daniel Weiss Associates, Inc.
33 West 17th Street
New York, NY 10011*

Cover art by Susan Tang

*Skylark Books is a registered trademark of Bantam Books, a
division of Bantam Doubleday Dell Publishing Group, Inc.
Registered in U.S. Patent and Trademark Office and elsewhere.*

*All rights reserved.
Copyright © 1992 by Francine Pascal.
Cover art and interior illustration copyright © 1992 by
Daniel Weiss Associates, Inc.
No part of this book may be reproduced or transmitted
in any form or by any means, electronic or mechanical,
including photocopying, recording, or by any information
storage and retrieval system, without permission in
writing from the publisher.
For information address: Bantam Books.*

*If you purchased this book without a cover you should be
aware that this book is stolen property. It was reported as
"unsold and destroyed" to the publisher and neither the author
nor the publisher has received any payment for this "stripped
book."*

ISBN 0-553-15924-0

Published simultaneously in the United States and Canada

Bantam Books are published by Bantam Books, a division of Bantam Doubleday Dell Publishing Group, Inc. Its trademark, consisting of the words "Bantam Books" and the portrayal of a rooster, is Registered in U.S. Patent and Trademark Office and in other countries. Marca Registrada. Bantam Books, 666 Fifth Avenue, New York, New York 10103.

PRINTED IN THE UNITED STATES OF AMERICA

OPM   0 9 8 7 6 5 4 3 2 1

To Jessica Ann Copskey

CHAPTER 1

A Surprise Guest

"Hurry up, Jess!" Elizabeth Wakefield called over her shoulder as she rushed into the den. "It's time for *Dr. Snapturtle's Animal Hour!*" She turned on the television and flopped down on the couch.

"Has it started yet?" asked her twin sister, Jessica, hurrying into the room.

"Not yet," Elizabeth replied. "We're just in time."

It was easy to tell that Elizabeth and Jessica were twins. They both had blue-green eyes and long blond hair with bangs.

They were the only identical twins in the second grade at Sweet Valley Elementary, and it was almost impossible for most people to tell them apart.

Jessica and Elizabeth were identical on the outside, but their personalities were as different as night and day. Elizabeth liked reading and playing soccer. Jessica preferred playing with her dollhouse and talking to her friends. But being different on the inside didn't stop them from being best friends.

One thing that the twins could always agree on was their favorite television show. They both loved *Dr. Snapturtle's Animal Hour.* The show was about animals, and it was hosted by a veterinarian named Dr. Snapturtle. He was Elizabeth's hero, because he was always making sick and injured animals better. He was very cheerful, and he loved to tell jokes on the show. Dr. Snapturtle had a dog named Duke, who was always on the show with him. Duke was a Dalmation, and the twins thought he was the best dog in the world.

"It's starting," Elizabeth exclaimed as the theme music began and Dr. Snapturtle walked out onto the stage with Duke right behind him.

"Welcome to the *Animal Hour*," Dr. Snapturtle said with a smile. "Duke and I have a great show for you today. Our first guest will be the big cats keeper from the Sweet Valley Zoo. After that, we'll meet some amazing sea creatures from the San Francisco Aquarium. Sounds great, doesn't it, Duke?"

Duke looked up at Dr. Snapturtle. He barked twice and wagged his tail.

"Thanks for reminding me, Duke," the vet

3

said with a laugh. "Duke wants me to tell you all that we'll also have a very special guest joining us a little later in the show. So don't go away, anybody. We'll be back in a moment."

A commercial came on. "I wonder who the special guest will be," Elizabeth said.

"I hope it's a baby animal," Jessica replied. "The baby rabbits he had on last week were so cute!"

"I love all the animals on the show," Elizabeth said. "Especially Duke."

"Me, too," Jessica replied. "I can't believe that everyone doesn't like the *Animal Hour* as much as we do."

"What do you mean?" Elizabeth asked.

"The other day after Mrs. Otis told us about our class trip to see a taping of the show, I heard Caroline Pearce telling Julie

Porter and Andy Franklin that Dr. Snapturtle is a big phony. She said he's not even a real vet, and that only babies watch the *Animal Hour*."

"That's not true," Elizabeth said angrily. "She'll see when she meets Dr. Snapturtle in person."

"The show's coming on again," Jessica said, leaning closer to the TV. "Don't worry. Caroline Pearce is just a big know-it-all."

Elizabeth forgot all about Caroline Pearce as she settled back to watch the *Animal Hour*. First, a woman from the zoo came on and talked about her job as a zookeeper. She described some of the things she had to do to take care of the lions, tigers, leopards, and other animals she worked with. Then she brought out a lynx from the zoo. It looked like an overgrown housecat with tufted ears.

5

After that, some people from the San Francisco Aquarium brought out a big tank full of colorful sea horses. The aquarium workers talked about all the special tanks that the aquarium had for different kinds of sea life.

Finally, after the last commercial break, Dr. Snapturtle announced that it was time to meet his extra-special guest.

One of Dr. Snapturtle's assistants brought out a bundle wrapped in a blanket and handed it to Dr. Snapturtle. When the vet pulled back the edge of the blanket, a tiny, round-eyed, whiskery face peeked out.

Elizabeth gasped. "A baby seal!"

"This little fellow was found orphaned on the beach," Dr. Snapturtle explained. "He was suffering from malnutrition and shock. One of his flippers is broken. We're doing ev-

6

erything we can to make him well, but he's still very sick. Keep your fingers crossed that he gets well soon."

Duke barked and wagged his tail again.

"Well, Duke is telling me that's all the time we have for today," Dr. Snapturtle said. "I'll see you next time, and remember, always be kind to animals."

"We will," Elizabeth and Jessica both said at once.

For once, Elizabeth didn't really mind that the show was over. After all, she would get to see the next episode of *Dr. Snapturtle's Animal Hour* in person!

CHAPTER 2

TV Tour

One week later, Jessica and Elizabeth lined up with the rest of their class to get on the bus for the class trip. "Let's sit in the middle today," Jessica said.

"OK." Elizabeth was holding her autograph book in one hand. She could hardly wait to meet Dr. Snapturtle.

The twins sat down together in a seat near their friends Amy Sutton and Eva Simpson. Eva leaned forward to talk to the twins. "This trip is going to be so much fun," she said. "I love the *Animal Hour*. I watch it every week."

"So do we," Elizabeth replied, smiling. "Dr. Snapturtle is the best."

Charlie Cashman got on the bus just in time to hear her. "I don't know why you're all so excited about that dumb show," he said loudly. "Only babies watch it."

Jessica made a face at Charlie. "You don't have to come on this trip if you don't want to."

"Don't pay any attention to him. He's just a spoilsport," said Lila Fowler. She sat down in the seat behind the twins.

Ellen Riteman sat down next to Lila. "Caroline Pearce says that Dr. Snapturtle isn't a real vet," she said. "Do you think he is?"

"I know he is," Elizabeth replied. "He

10

saves all kinds of animals when they're sick or hurt."

Just then, Caroline Pearce got on the bus. "Hey, Caroline, is it true that Dr. Snapturtle's a phony?" Ellen asked her.

"I'm sure of it," Caroline replied. "What kind of a name is Dr. Snapturtle? That's not a real name, and I bet he's not a real vet. He's just an actor pretending to be a vet." She walked toward the back of the bus.

Jessica shrugged. "I still think Liz is right. If Dr. Snapturtle weren't a real vet, he wouldn't be able to make all those animals well again. Like that cute little baby seal he had on last week."

The others nodded. "Do you think he'll ask for volunteers from the audience?" Eva asked.

"If he does, I'm definitely going to raise my

11

hand!" Jessica said. "I love being on TV." Jessica and Elizabeth had both been on TV twice before, once in a TV movie and once on the evening news.

"What if he asks you to hold a snake?" Ellen asked with a giggle.

"I would even do that," Jessica said, trying not to frown at the idea. She hoped there wouldn't be any snakes on the show that day.

Elizabeth laughed. She could tell what her twin was thinking. She knew Jessica hated anything scaly or slimy. "Have you ever met Dr. Snapturtle before?" she asked Amy. Amy's mother worked at the TV station, so Amy got to meet a lot of the other people who worked there.

"Yes, I met him once," Amy said. "He's nice. He tells lots of funny jokes, even when he's not on TV."

Elizabeth smiled. "You can tell he's nice just by watching him on the show. All the animals love him, especially Duke."

"What kinds of animals do you think will be on today?" said Lila.

"I hope the baby seal is on again," Elizabeth said.

"Me, too," said Ellen. "It's the cutest animal I ever saw."

A few minutes later the bus pulled into the station parking lot.

"We're here!" Elizabeth exclaimed.

Amy's mother, Mrs. Sutton, met the class in the front lobby. "Welcome to WSV-TV," she said. "I'll give you a short tour of the station before we go into the studio to watch the *Animal Hour.* Are there any questions before we get started?"

Elizabeth raised her hand. "Will we be

14

able to get Dr. Snapturtle's autograph?" she asked.

Charlie snickered. "I'll feed Duke your autograph book, so you can get his teeth prints."

"Dr. Snapturtle will be glad to sign autographs and answer any questions you have for him," Mrs. Sutton said, giving Charlie a stern look.

The first thing Mrs. Sutton showed the class was the videotape library. She explained that the library contained tapes of all the shows ever broadcast at the station. "This way, we can see what we've already done, or we can repeat a show that was popular," she said.

Jessica read the labels on the nearest shelf. "Look! Tapes of the *Animal Hour*. There are hundreds of them! Are the au-

15

dience volunteers for each show on these tapes, too?"

"They certainly are," Mrs. Sutton said.

Jessica smiled. More than anything, she wanted to be chosen to appear on television. She couldn't think of anything more exciting than appearing on her favorite TV show, especially now that she knew it might even be played more than once.

Next Mrs. Sutton explained how television signals travel through the air and into everyone's homes. She took the class into several small studios where talk shows were taped. Then they went into the news studio. Mrs. Sutton pointed to a large green screen.

"When you see the weather report with maps and symbols for rain and sun, this is what you're looking at," Mrs. Sutton said. "The maps show up on your TV, but the weather reporter, Teresa Cabrera, only sees the blank green screen."

"How does she know where to point?" Todd Wilkins asked.

"There's a monitor out of sight of the camera that shows her the pictures," Mrs. Sutton explained.

From somewhere in another part of the building, Jessica heard a bark. "Is that Duke?" she asked.

"Yes it is," Mrs. Sutton said. "Our last stop is the *Animal Hour* studio. Is everyone ready?"

"Yes," shouted several kids at once.

Elizabeth and Jessica looked at each other and grinned. They were ready!

CHAPTER 3

Applause, Applause

Elizabeth could hardly believe that she was in the *Animal Hour* studio. She sat down beside Jessica and looked around. Overhead lights hung from the ceiling and shone on the set. Elizabeth could hear her friends chattering all around her, but she was too excited to say anything.

Soon, the theme music began, and a red neon sign flashed the word "APPLAUSE." Elizabeth didn't need a sign to tell her to applaud. She clapped so hard that her hands hurt.

"Here he comes," Jessica whispered.

Dr. Snapturtle walked out onto the stage with Duke at his side. Elizabeth clapped even harder.

"Hello, and welcome to the *Animal Hour*," the vet said. "We have a great show for you today, don't we, Duke?"

Elizabeth leaned forward in her seat. Dr. Snapturtle's voice sounded a lot quieter than it did on TV. He also didn't seem to be smiling as much as he usually did. Elizabeth wondered if that was because things looked different on TV than they did in person.

"I'd like to say hello to the kids from Mrs. Otis's class," Dr. Snapturtle continued. "They're in the audience today." Everyone clapped again. "Our first guest on this week's show is our national symbol," Dr. Snapturtle said as an assistant walked onto the stage. A large bird was perched on the assistant's arm.

"It's an eagle," Elizabeth whispered, her eyes wide.

"This is an American bald eagle," Dr. Snapturtle explained. "She was found in her nest with a broken wing. She's being raised in as natural a setting as possible, so that we can release her back into the wild when she's big enough."

Elizabeth listened eagerly as Dr. Snapturtle continued to talk about eagles. She was thrilled to be watching the vet in person. He still didn't seem quite as cheerful to her as usual, but Elizabeth didn't mind. She was looking forward to meeting him and getting his autograph.

"Our next guest is a fellow I think you'll

21

like," Dr. Snapturtle said. He opened a door at the back of the stage, and a tiny, black pig trotted out.

"It's so cute!" Elizabeth whispered to Jessica.

"It's so little!" Jessica whispered back.

"This is a pygmy pig," Dr. Snapturtle said, picking up the animal. The pig raised its head to sniff the vet's face, and then it stuck out its small pink tongue and licked Dr. Snapturtle on the chin.

"Pygmy pigs are becoming very popular as pets," Dr. Snapturtle said. "They don't make people sneeze the way dogs and cats sometimes do. They're very smart and easy to train, and believe it or not, they are very clean."

"Wow, that would be a great pet!" Jessica whispered to Elizabeth.

28-3

Elizabeth nodded. "Especially since Dad and Steven are allergic to cats."

Dr. Snapturtle continued to talk about pigs for a few minutes, and then there was a commercial break. Elizabeth hoped that he would stay onstage during the commercials so that they could ask him questions. But he walked quickly off as soon as the cameras stopped running.

"Does Dr. Snapturtle seem different to you?" Elizabeth asked Jessica.

"No," Jessica answered. "I didn't notice anything different about him."

Elizabeth frowned. Maybe it was her imagination. The sign over their heads began to blink "APPLAUSE" again, and Dr. Snapturtle walked back onstage, leading a sleek black otter on a leash. The vet was carrying a bucket in his other hand.

"Now," he said. "I need a volunteer."

"ME!" Jessica yelled, jumping up from her seat and waving both hands in the air.

Elizabeth giggled. She could tell Jessica really wanted to be on TV!

"You look enthusiastic, young lady," Dr. Snapturtle said, pointing to Jessica. "Come on down."

Jessica ran down toward the stage with a big grin on her face. She climbed the steps onto the stage and stood next to Dr. Snapturtle. She waved at Elizabeth.

"This is a California sea otter," Dr. Snapturtle said, turning to Jessica. "And this is a bucket of raw fish."

Jessica made a face as she looked into the bucket. "Do you want me to hold the otter's leash?" she asked eagerly.

Dr. Snapturtle smiled a little. "No, you get to hold the raw fish!"

CHAPTER 4

Something Fishy

Jessica felt her cheeks turn pink as she stared down at the bucket and then at Dr. Snapturtle.

"What's your name?" the vet asked.

"Jessica," she said, swallowing hard.

"Welcome to the show, Jessica. Just pick up a fish and hand it to the otter," he said.

"OK," Jessica said, trying to look cheerful. She was on TV, but it was hard not to grimace when she reached into the bucket. The fish were cold and slimy, and they smelled awful. She had touched fish before on a family fishing trip, but that didn't mean she liked it.

She picked up a fish between her thumb and index finger and then held it out to the otter. The otter stood up on its hind legs and reached for the fish with its front paws. Jessica let go of the fish and snatched her hand away. "Yuck," she said with a shiver.

All of her classmates laughed, and Jessica felt even more embarrassed.

"Thank you, Jessica. You're a good sport," Dr. Snapturtle said, turning to the cameras. "That wraps up our show for today. Thanks for watching. And remember, always be kind to animals."

Jessica turned to smile at the camera, too, and then felt the otter sniff her hand. "Yikes!" she yelped.

Everyone laughed again. "We're clear!" said one of the station workers.

"Kids, you can see this show on TV this afternoon," said the show's director. "Thanks for coming to the taping."

"Come on down and meet the doctor now," Mrs. Otis said to the class.

Jessica tried wiping her hands on her pants, but she could still smell the fishy odor. In a moment, she and Dr. Snapturtle were surrounded by her classmates.

"You sure looked funny, Jessica," Lila said.

"Ha ha," Jessica said in a grumpy voice.

Elizabeth walked up to Dr. Snapturtle. "Could you please sign my autograph book? This is my favorite show."

"Of course," he said, not looking at her. He

signed her book quickly, and then picked up the otter in his arms.

"How's the baby seal?" Elizabeth wanted to know. "Did you fix its broken flipper?"

Dr. Snapturtle didn't seem to hear her. He patted the otter and then started to sign more autographs.

Elizabeth looked at her sister with a see-what-I-mean look.

Jessica nodded. Dr. Snapturtle was definitely not as friendly as he usually was on TV. Maybe he wasn't as nice a person as he seemed, she thought. He wasn't listening very closely to anyone's questions.

"Time to go, class," Mrs. Otis said after a few minutes. "Thank you so much, Doctor. We all had a wonderful time."

"You're welcome," the vet said with a small nod.

31

Talking and laughing, the class trooped out of the television studio and into the lobby.

"You're a TV star, Jessica," Charlie said, laughing at her.

"Jessica, the animal trainer," Jerry McAllister teased.

"Oh, be quiet," Jessica said.

As they began to file onto the bus, Jessica suddenly realized that she had forgotten something.

"I think I left my jacket somewhere in the TV station," she told her teacher. "Can I go back with Elizabeth to look for it?"

"Yes, but hurry up, girls," Mrs. Otis said, looking at her watch. "Try to be back here in five minutes."

CHAPTER 5

Harsh Words

Elizabeth and Jessica hurried back inside the station. "Do you remember where you left it?" Elizabeth asked.

"No, I just know I had it when we came in," Jessica said. She opened the door of the news broadcasting studio and peeked in. Camera operators were moving the large video cameras around on wheels, and someone was testing the overhead lights. "I don't see it anywhere," she whispered.

"Kids, we're about to start here. I'm afraid

you'll have to leave," said a man with a clip-board.

"Come on," Elizabeth said, backing up. "Let's try someplace else."

"I know," Jessica said. "I bet I left it on my seat in the *Animal Hour* studio when I got up to volunteer."

"We'll have to sneak in quietly," Elizabeth whispered. "They might be taping another show in there or something."

The twins tiptoed to the door of the *Animal Hour* studio.

"I'm sure it's in here," Jessica said, pushing open the door carefully.

They looked in. The studio was empty, but the lights were still on. The bucket of fish was onstage. It had tipped over, and a piece of fish had spilled out.

"Come on," Elizabeth whispered.

As the twins stepped inside the studio, they heard loud voices coming from offstage.

"I don't care whose fault it is," someone shouted. "It shouldn't have happened."

Elizabeth glanced quickly at Jessica. "That's Dr. Snapturtle's voice," she whispered.

"We've had this problem before!" he went on. "I don't want it to happen again!"

Elizabeth felt a sinking sensation in her stomach. She couldn't believe that someone as kind and cheerful as Dr. Snapturtle could sound so angry. He always seemed so patient and understanding on TV.

"Hurry up," she whispered, grabbing Jessica's hand.

They hurried up to the seats where they had watched the show. "Here's my jacket," Jessica said, leaning over to pick it up.

As they were about to leave, Dr. Snapturtle walked onto the stage. Duke was trotting behind him, wagging his tail. Then, halfway across the stage, Duke stopped and sniffed. His tail started to wag even harder. He walked over to the piece of fish and picked it up in his mouth.

Dr. Snapturtle turned around and saw what Duke was doing. "Put that down!" he yelled.

Duke dropped the fish. He put his tail between his legs, lowered his head, and looked up at Dr. Snapturtle with his large brown eyes.

Elizabeth froze. Duke was only doing something natural for a dog. There was no reason for Dr. Snapturtle to scold him so strongly.

"That was mean," she finally blurted out.

Dr. Snapturtle glanced up and noticed them for the first time. He still looked impatient and angry.

Elizabeth stared at him, and tears came to her eyes. He wasn't as friendly and kind to animals as he acted on TV, after all.

Jessica was thinking the same thing. "You *are* a big fake!" she yelled at him.

Then Jessica and Elizabeth dashed out of the studio together.

CHAPTER 6

Disappointment

"You won't believe what we just saw," Jessica said to her friends as the bus pulled out of the station parking lot.

Elizabeth didn't say anything. She looked very sad.

"What happened?" Caroline asked. She leaned forward from her seat across the aisle, looking curious. "Did you see someone famous?"

"No!" Jessica said in her most dramatic voice. "It was Dr. Snapturtle. He's really a mean man!"

"What are you talking about?" Amy demanded.

"We went back to the *Animal Hour* studio to get my jacket," Jessica explained. "Dr. Snapturtle was yelling and shouting and being mean to Duke."

Everyone looked surprised and disappointed, except for Caroline. "See?" she said with a satisfied smile. "I told you he was a big phony."

Jessica hated to admit it, but she was beginning to believe that Caroline had been right all along. Dr. Snapturtle wasn't the kind, patient person he pretended to be. Hadn't she heard him yelling at Duke with her very own ears? And hadn't he made her look silly by asking her to hold the raw fish? When Jessica sniffed her fingers, she could still smell it.

Todd Wilkins shook his head. "I can't believe it. I thought he was such a great guy."

Caroline looked around with her know-it-all smile. "I bet I'm right that he isn't even a vet," she said.

Mrs. Otis was listening to the conversation. "Now, wait a minute," the teacher interrupted seriously. "I'm sure there's a very good reason why Dr. Snapturtle lost his temper."

Jessica nodded. "The reason is, he's mean."

"But he's got to be a real vet," Elizabeth said. "He really does take care of sick animals and make them better, doesn't he?"

"Of course he's a real vet," Mrs. Otis reassured her.

"A real *mean* vet," Jessica said.

Mrs. Otis frowned. "Jessica, you know it's not right to jump to conclusions. Just because he was angry doesn't mean he isn't a vet, or even that he isn't a nice man."

Jessica didn't answer. She had changed her mind completely about Dr. Snapturtle. She knew she would never believe in him again.

When they got home, Jessica and Elizabeth ate their cookies and sipped their milk in silence.

"Didn't you have fun on your class trip?" Mrs. Wakefield asked finally. "You were really excited this morning."

"Yes," Elizabeth whispered, staring into her milk.

"No," Jessica answered. "Dr. Snapturtle is a fake. He yelled at Duke."

"Oh, I can't believe that he's a fake," Mrs.

Wakefield said. "He's had the show for so many years now. Everyone loves him. Even I do."

"Well, we don't like him anymore," Jessica said. "But I did get to be on the show." She smiled as she remembered that she would be on TV. Then she frowned as she remembered that she would be holding a raw fish and looking dumb.

Elizabeth opened her autograph book and stared at Dr. Snapturtle's signature. The expression on her face was so unhappy and disappointed that Jessica felt unhappy, too. She knew that Dr. Snapturtle had been Elizabeth's hero. Now it was obvious that he didn't deserve to be admired at all.

"The show will be on in a few minutes, girls," their mother said. "Why don't you take your snacks into the den?"

43

"I'm not going to watch," Elizabeth said in a low voice.

"Me neither," Jessica said immediately.

Their mother looked surprised. "Now, girls, Dr. Snapturtle is a good man. Why don't you give him a second chance? Anyway, don't you want to see yourself on TV, Jessica?"

"Well . . . sort of," Jessica said. She dunked a cookie into her milk and glanced over at Elizabeth. She knew how Elizabeth felt about Dr. Snapturtle. But she did want to see herself on television. "I guess I'll watch," she decided. She looked at Elizabeth. "But I won't enjoy it. I promise."

CHAPTER 7

A Surprise Visitor

At the beginning of the last class the next day, Mrs. Otis made an announcement.

"We won't do any geography today," she said, standing by the blackboard. "Instead, we're having a guest. Dr. Snapturtle called me this morning. He's coming by to explain what happened yesterday after the show. He feels very bad about it."

"The big phony," Jessica muttered under her breath.

Charlie looked over at Caroline and spoke

in a loud whisper. "He just doesn't want everyone to find out he's a fake and stop watching the show."

"I doubt that very much, Charlie," Mrs. Otis said. "I understand why you all feel disappointed. However, I do expect each of you to give Dr. Snapturtle a chance to explain."

Jessica turned to Lila and muttered, "I still say he's a two-faced meanie, no matter what his excuse is."

Lila nodded. "I think Caroline's right. He's not a real vet. It's all a lie," she whispered. "I bet he doesn't even *like* animals."

Ken Matthews heard her and leaned over. "He probably only hosts the *Animal Hour* because he gets lots of money for it," he added. "Can you believe he's coming here to try and convince us that he feels bad about being such a jerk?"

Elizabeth stared down at her desk. She couldn't guess what Dr. Snapturtle would say that would make her feel the same way about him again. Still, she was willing to listen, even if no one else in the class was.

A moment later, there was a knock on the door. Mrs. Otis went to open it, and Dr. Snapturtle walked into the classroom. He was greeted by complete silence.

"Hi, kids," he said, giving them a hopeful smile. "I know I got caught at a bad time yesterday, so I want to tell you all why I was in such a bad mood."

"He was in a bad mood because he hates animals," Caroline whispered to Sandy Ferris.

Dr. Snapturtle looked right at Caroline. "I don't hate animals at all," he said gently. "I love animals, and I've spent all of my life trying to take care of them."

"You didn't act like you loved Duke yesterday," Jessica said.

"Duke is my best friend," the vet replied. "But don't you sometimes get mad at your best friend, Jessica?"

Jessica didn't answer.

"Some of you might have seen last week's show," he went on patiently, "and the orphan baby seal we rescued."

Elizabeth felt her heart begin to thump inside her chest. Dr. Snapturtle sounded so serious that she could tell something bad had happened.

"We tried so hard to give that baby a chance," Dr. Snapturtle said. "I really

48

thought he was going to pull through. But yesterday, just before we began the show, one of my assistants told me that the seal had died."

Nobody in the class said a word. Elizabeth's eyes filled up with tears. She could remember exactly what the baby seal had looked like. It was hard to believe that it had died.

"I didn't have a chance to get over the shock," Dr. Snapturtle said, sitting on the edge of Mrs. Otis's desk and folding his arms. "All through the show, I was thinking about the seal and wondering what I did wrong. It distracted me and made me very impatient. That's why I got mad at Duke."

Elizabeth raised her hand. "But Duke didn't do anything wrong," she said softly.

"I know that," Dr. Snapturtle said. "But

we often lose our tempers with the ones we love, and it's usually when they don't deserve it at all."

The more Elizabeth thought about that, the more she realized it was true. She certainly lost her temper with Jessica from time to time, but that didn't mean she didn't love her sister.

She looked at Dr. Snapturtle. She was beginning to understand that he was a human being like anyone else, and he wasn't perfect.

She was also beginning to understand that she'd been right when she thought he was a good person. She knew now that he *did* love animals—especially Duke. "I think he's telling the truth," she whispered to Jessica.

Jessica turned to her and shook her head. "I don't."

CHAPTER 8

The Accident

"I still think he's a fake," Jessica whispered to Elizabeth. "He didn't have to be so mean to Duke, no matter what."

"Are there any more questions I can answer for you?" Dr. Snapturtle asked the class. He looked sad and tired. "Any questions at all?"

Nobody said anything. Dr. Snapturtle looked at Mrs. Otis and gave her a worried smile. "I have to go now. Thank you for letting me come. I hope I've straightened things out here."

"Thank you, Doctor," Mrs. Otis said, walking him to the door. "I'm sure you have."

It was almost time for the final bell to ring. Jessica began taking her books out of her desk and putting them into her tote bag.

"It's really sad that the seal died," she said.

"I bet he made up that whole story," Lila said.

"I bet you're right," Ellen agreed. "He just needed an excuse for being so mean and grouchy."

"Can we line up for our buses, Mrs. Otis?" Winston Egbert asked.

The teacher glanced at the clock. "All right. Have a nice afternoon and please try to understand why Dr. Snapturtle behaved the way he did. It's never easy to have one of your patients die when you're a doctor."

Jessica walked out into the hall. "Look, there he goes," she said, nudging Elizabeth with her elbow.

Dr. Snapturtle was walking slowly down the hallway toward the parking lot door.

"What a phony," Jessica said. Deep down, though, she wasn't quite as positive anymore.

Elizabeth shook her head. "I know he's a real vet, and I know he was just sad yesterday. I believe what he said."

They walked out onto the sidewalk. The school buses were lining up at the curb, and parents were pulling up in cars to take their kids to music lessons, softball practice, and other after-school activities.

Before Jessica could answer her sister, there was a squeal of tires and a high-pitched yelp.

"A dog's been hit!" someone yelled.

"Someone call the police," a crossing guard shouted.

"Come on!" Elizabeth said. She started running.

Jessica raced after her sister. A crowd was gathered by the side of the street. A woman was getting out of her car. She looked frightened and upset.

"I didn't see it! It just ran out in front of me!" she cried out. "I couldn't help hitting it!"

In the street, a small, brown dog was lying on its side. One leg was twisted at a strange angle, and the dog was panting weakly.

Elizabeth took one look at the injured dog and turned around. "I'm going to get Dr. Snapturtle," she said.

Jessica grabbed her arm. "What if he isn't really a vet?" she asked anxiously.

"He is," Elizabeth said. "I know he is." Without another word, she ran toward the parking lot as fast as she could.

Jessica glanced once more at the injured dog, and then chased after Elizabeth. "I hope he's not gone yet," she wished out loud.

She caught up with Elizabeth just as she reached Dr. Snapturtle's car. He had already started the engine and was about to back out of the parking space.

"Dr. Snapturtle!" Elizabeth yelled. "Wait! We need you!"

"Whoa!" he said in surprise as the twins skidded to a stop beside his open car window. "Be careful, kids."

"Dr. Snapturtle, you have to come quickly!" Elizabeth said.

"A dog got hit by a car in front of the school," Jessica added, breathing hard. She closed her eyes. If Dr. Snapturtle admitted now that he wasn't really a vet, he wouldn't be able to save the dog. Maybe he really didn't care about animals, in spite of what he said. She held her breath and waited for him to say, "No."

CHAPTER 9

A True Hero

"Where is the dog?" the vet asked, turning off the car engine.

"Out in front of the school," Elizabeth explained. "Please, you have to hurry!"

Dr. Snapturtle opened his door and grabbed a black bag that was sitting on the seat beside him. "Lead the way," he said, climbing out of the car.

They all started to run. When they reached the front of the school, Dr. Snapturtle raced out into the street. Elizabeth and Jessica were right behind him.

The crowd was even larger now, and some of the smaller children were crying. Some teachers were there, trying to keep the kids away from the injured dog, and everyone was talking at once.

"Let me through, please," Dr. Snapturtle said in a loud, firm voice.

While Elizabeth and Jessica and the others watched, the vet kneeled down in the street beside the dog. The dog whimpered and tried to move, but it couldn't. Elizabeth felt her stomach do a flip-flop. She knew the dog must be in pain.

"There, there," Dr. Snapturtle whispered to the injured animal. "I'm not going to hurt you."

He carefully felt the dog's leg, and stroked its head when it whined. Then he opened his bag and took out some bandages.

"This leg is broken," he said. "I'll have to take him to my clinic."

Elizabeth watched in anxious silence as the vet examined the dog's leg. As he worked, he talked quietly and soothingly to the injured animal. Little by little, the dog stopped whining and looked at Dr. Snapturtle with large, trusting eyes. It knew by instinct not to be afraid of the gentle, helpful man. When she saw how the dog trusted Dr. Snapturtle, Elizabeth knew that she had been right to believe in him. She knew that he really did love animals, and they loved him back.

Quickly but carefully, Dr. Snapturtle placed a wooden splint on the dog's leg and wrapped it with bandages. Then he took a hypodermic needle from his bag, wiped off a spot of skin with a cotton ball, and gave the dog a shot. The dog didn't even wince.

"That should help with the pain," the vet explained as he gathered the dog up in his arms. "Does anyone know whose animal this is?" he asked, looking around at the crowd.

"He hangs around here a lot," a fifth-grade boy said. "He doesn't have a collar. I don't know where he lives."

"I'll try to find out if he belongs to anyone," Dr. Snapturtle said. "But for now, I'll take him to my clinic. He may have some internal injuries, too, and I'll have to do a full examination."

Jessica looked up at Dr. Snapturtle with a mixture of surprise and relief on her face. "You really are a real vet, aren't you?"

"Yes, I am," he said, smiling. "I'm sorry you didn't believe me before. But I'm glad you trusted me enough to come and get me and give me a chance to prove it to you—and to help this dog."

"It was Liz's idea," Jessica admitted.

Elizabeth smiled at the doctor. He was definitely still her hero.

"Thanks, Liz," Dr. Snapturtle said. "Helping animals is what I love to do."

"Thank *you*," Elizabeth replied. She looked at the dog and began to feel nervous again. "Will you be able to save his life?"

Dr. Snapturtle looked down at the dog in his arms. The shot was beginning to take effect, and the dog was slowly closing its eyes.

"I think I will," the vet said softly. "I don't want to lose any more patients."

While everyone watched, Dr. Snapturtle carried the dog back to the parking lot and

carefully put it in his car. Elizabeth waved as the vet drove away.

"Wow," Jessica said, her eyes wide with admiration. "I'm glad he was here."

"Me, too," Elizabeth whispered.

CHAPTER 10

Saved

That night at dinner, Jessica and Elizabeth told the rest of the family about the emergency at school.

"It's lucky that Dr. Snapturtle was there," said Mrs. Wakefield.

"Is the dog going to live?" asked Steven, the twins' older brother.

"Yes," Jessica said firmly. "Dr. Snapturtle said he'd do everything he can."

Elizabeth licked the last bit of ice cream off her spoon. "I used to think I wanted to be a vet, but now I'm not sure," she said. "I wouldn't want any of the animals I took care of to die."

"Sometimes it happens, honey," Mrs. Wakefield said gently. "No matter how good a doctor is, some animals are too sick or too hurt to survive. All a vet can do is try as hard as possible."

"That's what happened to the baby seal," Elizabeth agreed. "It was already too sick when it was brought to Dr. Snapturtle."

Jessica put her chin in her hands. "Remember when we found Misty and we were afraid she was going to die?"

Misty was the stray cat the twins had secretly kept in their bedroom. They hadn't told their parents about her because Mr. Wakefield and Steven were allergic to cats. But when Misty wouldn't eat anymore,

Jessica and Elizabeth had been so worried that they had told their mother.

"Misty was just going to have kittens," Elizabeth said with a smile. "That's the fun part of taking care of animals."

"I hope this means you'll start watching the *Animal Hour* again," Mr. Wakefield said. "I know Dr. Snapturtle must be a very special person."

Jessica nodded. "I'm not missing a single show. I wish I could volunteer again, too."

"Even if you had to hold smelly raw fish?" Elizabeth teased her.

"Sure!" Jessica said. "I'd do anything for Dr. Snapturtle, now. I'd even hold bugs."

"Me, too," Elizabeth said with a smile. She took a sip of her grape juice. "Maybe I *will* be a vet when I grow up, after all. Even if you can't save *all* of the animals you try to help, it must be nice to save some of them."

"Like that dog today," said Jessica.

Elizabeth nodded. "If I do become a vet, I just hope I'm as good as Dr. Snapturtle."

At school the next day, Mrs. Otis announced that she had some good news. "Dr. Snapturtle called this morning to say that the dog is doing just fine. He's sure it will make a complete recovery."

"Did they find the owner?" Amy asked.

"No," Mrs. Otis said. "The doctor thinks it's a stray. If no one claims it, it might end up being a regular on the show as a friend for Duke."

"Mrs. Otis?" Caroline asked, raising her hand. "Can we go on another trip to see the *Animal Hour*?"

Jessica stared at Caroline. Before the class trip Caroline hadn't liked Dr. Snapturtle at all. She certainly had changed her mind.

"We do have another class trip coming up soon," Mrs. Otis said. "But not to the TV station. It's time for our annual Field Day games up at Secca Lake."

In the front row, Andy Franklin raised his hand.

"Yes, Andy?" Mrs. Otis asked. Andy was one of the smartest students in the class.

Andy held up a book. "My book about UFOs says some people have seen UFOs at Secca Lake."

"Really?" Mrs. Otis asked with a surprised look.

Jessica and Lila both giggled. "Andy wants to meet a Martian," Jessica whispered to her friend.

"When we go to Secca Lake, can we look for signs of UFOs?" Andy asked, pushing his wobbly glasses up on his nose.

"Well," Mrs. Otis said in a doubtful voice, "we'll have to see about that."

"Right," said Charlie, laughing. "We'll have to see if the aliens want to take Andy away to another planet."

"Maybe they'll take *you*," Andy said angrily.

Is there any alien life at Secca Lake? Find out in Sweet Valley Kids #29, ANDY AND THE ALIEN.

SWEET VALLEY KIDS

Jessica and Elizabeth have had lots of adventures in *Sweet Valley High* and *Sweet Valley Twins*…now read about the twins at age seven! You'll love all the fun that comes with being seven—birthday parties, playing dress-up, class projects, putting on puppet shows and plays, losing a tooth, setting up lemonade stands, caring for animals and much more! It's all part of SWEET VALLEY KIDS. Read them all!

☐	SURPRISE! SURPRISE! #1	15758-2	$2.75/$3.25
☐	RUNAWAY HAMSTER #2	15759-0	$2.75/$3.25
☐	THE TWINS' MYSTERY TEACHER # 3	15760-4	$2.75/$3.25
☐	ELIZABETH'S VALENTINE # 4	15761-2	$2.75/$3.25
☐	JESSICA'S CAT TRICK # 5	15768-X	$2.75/$3.25
☐	LILA'S SECRET # 6	15773-6	$2.75/$3.25
☐	JESSICA'S BIG MISTAKE # 7	15799-X	$2.75/$3.25
☐	JESSICA'S ZOO ADVENTURE # 8	15802-3	$2.75/$3.25
☐	ELIZABETH'S SUPER-SELLING LEMONADE #9	15807-4	$2.99/$3.50
☐	THE TWINS AND THE WILD WEST #10	15811-2	$2.75/$3.25
☐	CRYBABY LOIS #11	15818-X	$2.99/$3.50
☐	SWEET VALLEY TRICK OR TREAT #12	15825-2	$2.75/$3.25
☐	STARRING WINSTON EGBERT #13	15836-8	$2.75/$3.25
☐	JESSICA THE BABY-SITTER #14	15838-4	$2.75/$3.25
☐	FEARLESS ELIZABETH #15	15844-9	$2.75/$3.25
☐	JESSICA THE TV STAR #16	15850-3	$2.75/$3.25
☐	CAROLINE'S MYSTERY DOLLS #17	15870-8	$2.75/$3.25
☐	BOSSY STEVEN #18	15881-3	$2.75/$3.25
☐	JESSICA AND THE JUMBO FISH #19	15936-4	$2.99/$3.50
☐	THE TWINS GO TO THE HOSPITAL #20	15912-7	$2.99/$3.50
☐	THE CASE OF THE SECRET SANTA (SVK Super Snooper #1)	15860-0	$2.95/$3.50
☐	THE CASE OF THE CHRISTMAS BELL (SVK Super Snooper #2)	15964-X	$2.99/$3.50

Bantam Books, Dept. SVK, 2451 S. Wolf Road, Des Plaines, IL 60018

Please send me the items I have checked above. I am enclosing $_____ (please add $2.50 to cover postage and handling). Send check or money order, no cash or C.O.D.s please.

Mr/Ms _____

Address _____

City/State _____ Zip _____

SVK-4/92

Please allow four to six weeks for delivery.
Prices and availability subject to change without notice.